# Inventors
## Making Things Better

Written by Andrew Clements

STECK-VAUGHN
ELEMENTARY · SECONDARY · ADULT · LIBRARY

A Harcourt Classroom Education Company

www.steck-vaughn.com

# Contents

## Inventors Solve Problems

**Inventors** are people who think a lot.
They are curious about how things work.
Inventors want to fix problems. They
want to make things better. Their
inventions make our lives better and
safer. This book tells about ten famous
inventors. It tells the questions they
asked and how they answered them.

## Keeping People Safe

**How could the police keep safe from bullets?** They cannot just catch bullets like Superman does in movies. Police officers needed a better way to keep safe from bullets. Then Stephanie Kwolek invented something very important.

After college, Kwolek got a job at a chemical company. There she invented many new things. Her most important invention was a special kind of **plastic**.

This plastic, called Kevlar®, is stronger than steel. It can be made into a vest for the police to wear. A Kevlar® vest is light, but it is strong enough to stop a bullet. Wearing the vest has helped save officers' lives.

A police officer wears a bulletproof vest.

How could we be safe from gas fires? In the 1940s, most planes, ships, and trucks used gasoline. At times, the gas could catch on fire. Water couldn't put out a gas fire. This kind of fire was very hard to put out. People were badly hurt in these fires.

Percy Lavon Julian loved to solve problems. He thought about the fire problem. He invented a **foam** spray. His foam stopped gas flames fast. The foam quickly covered the fire so air could not get to it. Without air, the fire could not burn. Foam spray saved many people's lives. Today, the foam spray is also used in many home **fire extinguishers**.

A fire extinguisher's foam spray puts out a fire.

## Moving People Around

How could we make cars faster and cheaper? The first cars were built one at a time. This took a long time and cost a lot of money. Only a few people could buy these cars.

Henry Ford started making cars in 1903. Many people wanted to buy them. He could not make cars fast enough. He needed to think of a better way.

Ford invented a new way to make cars. His idea was the **assembly line**. The cars moved along on belts in a line to the workers. Each worker added one part to the car. By the end of the line, the car was finished. Ford called it the Model T. Then Ford could sell more cars faster and for less money. Soon many more people bought cars.

Henry Ford invented the assembly line to build cars faster.

**How could people go to the top of very tall buildings?** Walking all the way up the stairs would be too hard to do. Many years ago, the first **elevators** were put in tall buildings. These elevators used ropes. Sometimes the ropes broke. The elevators crashed. They were not safe.

In 1853, Elisha Otis invented a safe elevator. His elevator stopped by itself. There was no more crashing if the ropes broke.

Safe Otis elevators have made it possible for people to build even taller buildings. Today, buildings can be over one hundred stories high!

Tall buildings must have safe elevators.

**How could the first airplane fly?** People have always wanted to fly like birds. But they needed a machine to help them fly. For many years, inventors had tried to make a flying machine. But no one had made it work.

In 1903, Orville and Wilbur Wright wanted to be able to fly anywhere. The two brothers invented an airplane with a motor on it. Their airplane flew for twelve seconds! That was longer than anyone else had ever flown.

Today, airplanes are the fastest way to travel. They can fly faster than 500 miles per hour. They can cross the ocean in less than four hours. Today, people can fly anywhere in the world on airplanes.

The Wright brothers flew the first airplane.

## Sending Messages

How could people write long messages to each other? Long ago, people wrote on bark, clay, and dried skins. But they couldn't write long messages. People needed something better to write on.

Over 1,000 years ago, Ts'ai Lun worked in China. The Emperor of China wanted everything written down. So Ts'ai Lun invented paper.

He mixed tiny bits of wood and cloth in water. Then he pulled the mix through a screen. When the bits dried, they formed a sheet of paper. This took him a long time to make. Today, machines make huge rolls of paper in a short time.

Paper is now made quickly by huge machines.

**How could people fix their writing mistakes?** In the past, people had to erase the mistakes or start over on a clean sheet of paper. This left messy pages.

Bette Nesmith Graham did not like to erase her mistakes. She thought there had to be a better way to fix them. She began mixing different **liquids** to cover her mistakes. She tried and tried. Finally she made a liquid that worked. Her mistakes just disappeared!

Soon many people wanted Graham's invention. She made millions of dollars on it. Today, people still use her invention to correct mistakes on paper.

Birthday Party!
at Lee's House
on April 15
from 2:00-4:00

Party!
louse
15
-4:00

Bette Nesmith Graham invented a liquid to fix mistakes.

How could we send messages to someone who is far away? The **telegraph** is a machine that sends words through electric wires. Each written word changes into little clicks.

Alexander Graham Bell had a better idea. He wanted electric wires to carry sounds. Then people who were far away could talk to each other. Bell worked with Thomas Watson. They invented the **telephone** in 1876. Bell had the idea, and Watson built the telephone.

Soon telephone wires were put up everywhere. Today, people can talk to each other anywhere.

Alexander Graham Bell invented the telephone.

How could we send pictures through the air? Vladimir Zworykin knew that sound went through air. He wondered if pictures could travel through the air, too.

Zworykin studied for many years. Then, in 1923, he invented a picture tube. It was like a television screen. Electric signals traveled through the air and made a picture on the screen.

Zworykin's invention made **television** possible. Many other inventors made other parts, so no one person is called the inventor of TV.

Today, we also have movie recorders and cam recorders. We can use them to make movies and watch them later.

Today we can make movies of special times.

Inventors help make our lives easier. They solve problems. They make us safer. They make work go faster.

You can be an inventor. What would you like to invent? Would it be something to help us send messages to each other? Would it be something to make us safer?

Look around you. Think about a problem. You might invent something that would help make the world a better place for everyone.

Inventors are working today to solve problems.

# Glossary

**assembly line**   a way of building cars in which workers do different parts

**elevator**   a machine that moves things up and down floors in a building

**fire extinguisher**   a tool that puts out fires

**foam**   something that puts out gas fires

**inventor**   someone who makes a new thing or a new way to do something

**liquid**   something that pours, such as water

**plastic**   a hard material that can be molded

**telegraph**   a machine for sending a code through wires

**telephone**   a machine for sending sound

**television**   a machine that gets sound and picture signals